Weekly Reader Children's Book Club presents

Basil Brush Gets a Medal

by Peter Firmin

Prentice-Hall, Inc.,
Englewood Cliffs, New Jersey

Copyright © 1973 by Kaye & Ward Ltd., London

First American edition published 1978 by
Prentice-Hall, Inc.

Printed in the United States of America   J

Prentice-Hall International, Inc., London
Prentice-Hall of Australia, Pty. Ltd., North Sydney
Prentice-Hall of Canada, Ltd., Toronto
Prentice-Hall of India Private Ltd., New Delhi
Prentice-Hall of Japan, Inc., Tokyo
Prentice-Hall of Southeast Asia Pte. Ltd., Singapore

Library of Congress Cataloging in Publication Data

Firmin, Peter.
    Basil Brush gets a medal.

    SUMMARY: Basil Brush gets a medal for being
such a helpful fox, and Harry gets a special gift
from the princess for being such a special mole.
    [1. Foxes—Fiction. 2. Moles (Animals)—
Fiction]   I. Title.
PZ7.F49873Bavg 1978   [E]   78-6108
ISBN 0-13-066688-2

**For Charlotte
and Sian**

Basil Brush is a helpful fox.
He tries to help others whenever he can.

He helps old people.

He helps children.

He helps animals and birds.
Basil Brush got a medal
for being so helpful.

Harry is a mole.
He tries to be helpful too.

Basil and Harry went to a palace.
In the palace lived a princess who had
a big box of medals.

She liked to give medals to people who
had done something very special.

There were other people waiting outside
the palace gates.
There was a very brave soldier.
There was a clever inventor.

There was an actress who had acted for
years on the stage and a nurse who had
saved many lives.

They had all come to get medals from the princess, and Basil had come for a medal, too, for being such a helpful fox.

"I've come for my medal," said Basil to
the gate-keeper. "Will you open the gate
with your key?"
"We've come for ours too," said all the
other people. "Why are we waiting so long?"

"I would open the gate if I could," said
the gate-keeper, "but I cannot open it yet."

13

"If you've lost your key," said Harry the
mole, "I've something here that might do.
It's a nail that I picked up on the road.
Could you open the gate with a nail?"

"Oh, I have the key," said the gate-keeper,
"but the gate must stay shut till the
princess is ready. She always has breakfast
before she gives medals, and she has no
fresh milk for her porridge.
When the farmer brings milk for the royal
porridge, then I may open the gate."

Basil and Harry went to the farm.
They went to see the farmer.

"The princess needs milk for her porridge,"
said Basil. "Will you send milk to the palace?"

"I would send milk for the royal porridge," said the farmer. "The milkmaids are waiting to milk the cows. But the cows have not come from the meadow."

Basil and Harry went up to the meadow.
They went to see the cowman.

"The milkmaids are waiting," Basil called.
"They are waiting to milk the cows.
The farmer needs milk
to take to the princess.
She has no fresh milk for her porridge.
Will you bring the cows to the farm?"

"I would bring the cows to the farm,"
said the cowman, "but the bridge is broken
and the cows cannot cross."

"If the bridge is broken," said Harry the
mole, "I have something here that might do.
It's a nail that I picked up on the road.
Could you mend the bridge with a nail?"

"We need more than a nail," the cowman said.
"We need wood to mend the bridge.
If you go to the forest and ask the woodman,
he will cut down a tree."

Basil and Harry went to the forest.
They went to see the woodman.

"The bridge is broken," Basil said.
"Will you please cut down a tree?
We need some wood to mend the bridge
for the cows to cross over
to go to the farm
to give fresh milk for the princess.
She has no milk for her porridge."

"I would cut down a tree,"
the woodman said, "but my axe is blunt
and my grindstone is dry."

"If your axe is blunt," said Harry the mole,
"I have something here that might do.
It's a nail that I picked up on the road.
Could you sharpen your axe with a nail?"

"A nail will not do," the woodman said.
"I need water for the grindstone.
I sent my wife to the well for water,
but she has not come back yet."

Basil and Harry went to the well.
They found the woodman's wife.

"Where is the water?" Basil said.
"Your husband needs water
to wet the grindstone to sharpen his axe,
to cut down a tree to mend the bridge.
The bridge must be mended
for the cows to cross over
to go to the farm
to give fresh milk for the princess.
She has no milk for her porridge."

"I would bring water," said the woodman's
wife, "but the handle is broken.
The well will not work!"

"If the handle is broken," said Harry the mole,
"I have something here that might do.
It's a nail that I picked up on the road.
Could you mend the well handle with a nail?"

"That nail *will* do," said Basil Brush.
"A nail is just the thing to mend
the handle of the well."

So the handle was mended.

The woodman had water.

The axe was sharpened.

The tree was cut down.

The bridge was mended.

The cows crossed over.

The milkmaids milked the cows.

The fresh milk was taken to the palace,
and the princess had milk for her porridge.

"Now I may open the gate," said the
gate-keeper, "and the princess will
give you your medals."
So he opened the gate, the people went
in, and the princess gave them all medals.

One for the soldier.

One for the inventor.

One for the actress and one for the nurse.

Basil Brush got a medal
for being so helpful.

Only Harry did not get a medal.

"Because you are such a special mole,"
said the princess,
"I will give you a special gift."
She gave Harry a silver bowl and a spoon.
"It's a gift for a helpful mole," she said.
"I do like fresh milk with my porridge."

THE END